For Evie, who is a little wild thing,
and for Buddy and all his friends
at Keinton Mandeville school – Jackie M.

For Tom and Hannah
and their brilliant Mum, Jackie – James M.

First published in Great Britain in 2005 by Frances Lincoln Children's Books,
4 Torriano Mews, Torriano Avenue, London NW5 2RZ

www.franceslincoln.com

Distributed in the USA by Publishers Group West

British Library Cataloguing in Publication Data
available on request

ISBN 1-84507-298-7

Set in Oneleigh

Printed in China

1 3 5 7 9 8 6 4 2

Can You See A Little Bear?

Written by James Mayhew

Illustrated by Jackie Morris

FRANCES LINCOLN CHILDREN'S BOOKS

Elephants are big,

mice are small,

Can you see **a little bear** standing on **a ball?**

Lions are yellow,   peacocks are blue,

Can you see **a little bear** trying on **a shoe?**

Snakes are thin,
a walrus is fat,

Can you see a little bear trying on a hat?

Parrots can be **green**

and parrots can be **red**,

Can you see **a little bear** standing on **his head?**

Giraffes are tall,

guinea-pigs are short,

Can you see the toy that a little bear has bought?

Whales can swim and seagulls fly,

Can you see a little bear flying very high?

Ducks like the rain,

penguins like the snow,

Here's Little Bear –
and he's putting on a show!

Chickens like the **day**,

foxes like

the night,

Can you see a big bear

carrying a light?

Camels like the **desert**,

dolphins like the **sea**,

Can you see **a little bear**

going home for **tea**?

Crocodiles cry

and kookaburras laugh,

Now it's time for Little Bear to have a little bath!

Deer can **run**...

and hares can **leap**...

I think **Little Bear** is almost fast asleep.

Cats like the sun
and owls like the moon,

Good night, Little Bear –
hope to see you soon!